Fox
Makes
Friends

Published by Bonney Press,
an imprint of Hinkler Books Pty Ltd
45–55 Fairchild Street
Heatherton Victoria 3202 Australia
www.hinkler.com.au

BONNEY
PRESS

Originally published by Fernleigh Books, London

Prepress: Graphic Print Group

ISBN: 978 1 7436 3503 2

Printed and bound in China

Fox
Makes
Friends

Adam Relf

BONNEY
PRESS

Fox sat in his room.
He was bored.
"I know," he said.
"I need a friend."

Fox picked up his net and went to see his mother.
"I'm going to catch a friend," he declared.
"You can't catch friends," Mother explained.
"You have to *make* friends."
So Fox put down his net and
set off to make a friend.

"What can I make a friend out of?"
he thought.
He picked up some sticks, an apple
and some nuts, and fixed them
all together. At last he had
a brand new friend standing
in front of him.

"Are you my friend?" Fox asked,
but the friend said nothing.
"Can you come and play?" he said,
but the friend didn't move. "Maybe he's
too small," Fox thought. "I need to make
a bigger friend!"

Just then a rabbit ran by.
"Excuse me," said Fox. "I'm trying
to make a friend but this one is
too small. Can you help me
make a bigger one?"
     "Okay," said Rabbit.

They worked together and picked up a turnip,
some tomatoes, and some twigs. They stuck
them all together and soon they had a bigger
friend standing before them.
"Will you be our friend?" they asked,
but there was no answer.

"Can you come and play?" they said,
but the friend just stood there.
"Maybe he's still too small,"
said Rabbit.

A moment later Fox and Rabbit
heard giggling in the treetops.
It was a squirrel.
"What a mess you two are
making!" he laughed.
"Well, if you can do
better, come down and
help us!" said Fox.
"Okay," said Squirrel.

This time all three of them set to work.
They picked up a huge pumpkin, a turnip,
some branches and some apples.
They put them all together and had
the biggest friend they could make.
"Are you our friend?" they asked.
"Please can you come and play?"
But there was no reply.

Finally they all gave up.
"Oh well," said Fox. "I suppose I will never be able to make a friend."

Just then Fox's mother
came by.
"Hello," she said. "Who are
all your new friends?"
"Oh," said Fox. "My plan
didn't work. We made friends
but they won't play with us."
"Not them!" giggled his mother.
"These friends!" she said,
pointing to Squirrel
and Rabbit.

Fox looked over at Squirrel and Rabbit, and suddenly understood that he had been making friends all along!

So Fox, Squirrel, and Rabbit
played for the rest of the day,
and they stayed friends forever.